'The noise came aga
Jenny looked at each
stood absolutely stil
and someone coughe
it could only be a fev
next bend. An engin

''Quick,'' whispered

Ignoring the brambles and nettles, the girls
pushed themselves into the hedge and crouched
behind a thick bush . . .'

Sarah's dad has disappeared, leaving behind him
a mysterious note. Together with her friend
Jenny, Sarah sets out to find him – and the two
girls are soon hot on the trail of some dangerous
criminals!

SCENT OF DANGER

SCENT OF DANGER

ROSEMARY HAYES

ILLUSTRATED BY KEVIN JONES

YEARLING BOOKS

SCENT OF DANGER

A YEARLING BOOK 0 440 862612

First published in Great Britain by Blackie and Son Ltd

PRINTING HISTORY

Blackie edition published 1989
Yearling edition published 1990

Text copyright © 1989 by Rosemary Hayes
Illustrations copyright © 1990 by Kevin Jones

This book is set in 14/16 pt Century Schoolbook
by Colset Private Limited, Singapore.

Yearling Books are published by Transworld Publishers Ltd.,
61-63 Uxbridge Road, Ealing, London W5 5SA, in Australia
by Transworld Publishers (Australia) Pty. Ltd., 15-23 Helles
Avenue, Moorebank, NSW 2170, and in New Zealand by
Transworld Publishers (N.Z.) Ltd., Cnr. Moselle and
Waipareira Avenues, Henderson, Auckland.

Made and printed in Great Britain by
The Guernsey Press Co. Ltd, Guernsey, Channel Islands.

For Alexander, Philippa and Oliver

Chapter One

It was nearly dinner-time. The sun streamed into the classroom and Miss Appleby was talking about the school play.

Sarah sat in the back row, chewing her pencil and watching a trapped fly buzz against the window; she was miles away.

'Sarah Jones, I'm talking to you!' Sarah's best friend, Jenny, nudged her and Sarah jumped. All the other children giggled. 'You haven't been listening, dear, have you?' said Miss Appleby.

Sarah looked down at her lap and shook her head. Miss Appleby sighed.

'I *said*, dear, that you have been chosen for the main part in the play.'

Sarah's mouth opened very wide and she blushed. Then she smiled.

She couldn't wipe the grin off her face. She smiled all through afternoon lessons until Jenny said if she didn't stop smirking she'd hit her. At last it was time to go home. Sarah grabbed her school bag and was first in the line for the school bus, jiggling from one foot to the other, waiting for everyone else to come. Why were they so *slow*?

The big bus throbbed as they got on and Sarah and Jenny sat on the seat nearest the door.

Sarah was on her feet long before the bus reached the end of her street and was halfway up the hill before it turned the next corner. She ran all the way home, her bag banging against her back. She couldn't *wait* to tell Mum the news; she'd never believe it!

She threw open the gate and ran

down the path. At the back door she stopped, her hand on the latch; Mum was probably in the garden. She glanced round the side of the wall. Then she saw her mother and all the excitement left her; the smile, which had been on her face for hours, disappeared and a familiar cold feeling returned.

Mum didn't see her. She was kneeling in the back garden and she had been weeding, but now her head was bent and Sarah knew she was crying again. Since Dad had left, she cried a lot.

Aggie, their terrier dog, was in the garden, too. She bounded over to Sarah. Sarah patted her, then let herself into the house, dropped her school bag on the kitchen floor and walked slowly into the living-room. Her little brother, James, was watching television. Sarah sat down beside him, not looking at the screen or hearing what was said.

A few minutes later, Mum came in:

'Hello love,' she said. 'Did you have a good day?'

Sarah nodded, but she said nothing about the play. She knew Mum wasn't really interested; not in the way she used to be. In the last few weeks, her mother had changed; there was a far-away look in her eyes and, as she spoke, she twisted her wedding ring round and round her finger.

There was nothing fancy for tea. Mum did her best, and there was always plenty to eat, but there was never any money for treats. Things had been bad before – Dad had been out of work for ages – but since he'd gone, they had even less to live on and the bills were mounting up all the time.

If only he'd come back, thought Sarah. If only we knew where he was.

She thought about Dad all the time. Why had he gone off? He hadn't even said goodbye. Her dad was gentle; he told her stories and made her laugh. Where was he? What was he doing?

James was always saying, 'When's Dad coming home. Why's he gone away?' And Mum's answer was always the same:

'He's gone to look for work, love. He'll be back soon.'

But Sarah knew this wasn't true.

Dad had disappeared on a Saturday, about three weeks ago. Mum, Sarah and James had been out at the park with Aggie, the dog, and when they got back to the house, Dad wasn't there.

At first, Mum didn't worry. They'd had tea, as usual, and Sarah sat down to watch television. But later, Mum went upstairs to fetch a toy for James and she didn't come down. After a while, Sarah went to ask her something. She found her in her bedroom, standing by the window crying, with a crumpled note in her hand.

'Whatever's the matter, Mum?'

Mum had dried her eyes and stuffed the note hurriedly into her pocket.

'Nothing, dear,' she'd said and wiped her eyes and smiled. But later, she said to Sarah and James, 'Dad has gone away for a little while to try and find some work. He'll be back as soon as he can.' But she didn't look at Sarah as she spoke, and all the time she twisted her wedding ring round and round her finger.

Sarah knew for certain that her mother was lying and she felt sick in her stomach. Mum never lied. Sarah said nothing, but after James had gone to bed and Mum was in the kitchen, she crept upstairs. She was determined to find the note that had upset Mum so much and, at last, she did.

It was in Dad's handwriting, but she couldn't believe that her Dad had written it. This is what it said:

'I can't stay in the house just now. I'll be in touch soon. Whatever you do, don't try and find me or go to the police. If you do, you will never see me again.'

All that had happened three weeks ago. Since then, there had been no news of Dad. Mum looked dreadful, but she kept pretending that Dad was away looking for a job. Sarah didn't tell Mum she'd found the note.

Sarah went to bed early that night. She still hadn't told Mum about the play, but it didn't seem important now. She wasn't really tired and she sat hunched in bed, hugging her knees and staring at the wall. Then she lay down and tried to sleep, but she couldn't. She tossed and turned for ages and, at last, gave up trying. She switched on the light, got out of bed and padded about her room.

She rearranged her teddies at the end of her bed, then she tried to read a book, but the words danced in front of her eyes and she couldn't concentrate. She threw it on the floor and walked over to the chest of drawers. On top, there was a photo of her with James and Mum and Dad; they were all smiling. She picked up the photo and stared at it. *Why* had he left them? Where was he and why didn't he get in touch? She felt the tears prick in her eyes and she wiped them away angrily with her hand, then she put the photo back and pulled open the drawer underneath.

Sarah rummaged underneath the neatly-stacked clothes until she found a package wrapped in tissue paper. Very carefully, she unwound the paper and took out a small, cheap address book. No one, not even Mum, knew she had it. Sarah had found it a few days ago, down the side of a chair in the living-room. There were only a few names and addresses in the book and they didn't mean anything to her, but it was Dad's writing, so it must belong to him.

Sarah took the book back to bed with her and slipped it under her pillow. She lay on her side and stroked the book with her thumb and finger; then suddenly she started crying and when, at last, the worst was over, she drifted into an uneasy sleep.

Sarah woke with a start. The dream had seemed so real that it took her a while to realize that it was only a dream. Her finger and thumb were still clutching Dad's address book and, in her half-sleeping, half-waking state, she thought, just for a moment, that Dad was standing in the room. Then she rubbed her eyes and the image was gone.

She sat up in bed, still holding the book. She had dreamt that she'd seen Dad. He was somewhere out in the country, among a crowd of people. She had waved and shouted to him and tried to reach him, but people kept coming between them. Every time she had pushed towards him, Dad had gone further and further away until he was just a figure in the distance. She'd tried to run, but her legs wouldn't move. She'd shouted: 'Wait for me! I'm coming!' But Dad had disappeared.

Sarah stumbled out of bed still holding the book. She turned the pages, reading the names and addresses by the weak light at the window. Would any of these people know where her dad had gone? The names meant nothing to her – but there were addresses and phone numbers; surely *someone* must know.

'I'm going to find him,' she whispered to the empty room. 'Somehow, I'm going to find my dad.'

Chapter Two

The next day was Saturday. In the morning, Sarah, Mum and James went shopping. Saturday morning shopping used to be fun when Dad had a job. They would all go off to the supermarket and Dad would pick things from the shelves and pop them into the basket when Mum wasn't looking. If James got bored, Dad used to take him out to the car park and play games with him, then, when the shopping was finished, they would load up the car and go off to the café for sticky cakes and cokes.

The car had been sold months ago and the visits to the café had stopped too. But somehow Dad had made the bus trip fun and he'd always been there to help carry the shopping.

This morning, James started whining even before they reached the bus stop:

'I don't want to go shopping!' He stamped his feet and pulled away when Sarah tried to take his hand.

'Come on James,' said Mum. Sarah could hear the weariness in her voice.

'If you're a good boy, I'll buy you some sweets,' said Sarah. James scowled, but he allowed himself to be towed along.

He was a nuisance at the supermarket, too. He roared up and down the aisles, picking things up and knocking things down, while Sarah and Mum looked for bargains. Mum noted the prices of everything, but even so they found they didn't have enough money when they reached the check-out, so they had to put a few things back on the shelves. Sarah blushed as the girl at the check-out sighed and drummed her bright red fingernails on the side of the cash-register, waiting for them to sort themselves out.

They heaved the supermarket bags onto the bus, then carried them all the way from the bus stop to the house. By the time they got home, Mum and Sarah were cross and tired and James was screaming. But Aggie gave them a noisy welcome – as if they'd been gone for a week.

When she'd helped unpack the shopping, Sarah went up to her room. She heard James and Mum go out into the garden, so she lay down on her bed, stared at the ceiling, and tried to think. She tried to remember the few days before Dad had dis-appeared. Had anything happened just before he left. Anything out of the ordinary? But, try as she might, she could think of nothing. Dad had just been Dad.

The address book was still under her pillow. She picked it up. It was her secret. She looked carefully through all the names and addresses again. Still they meant nothing to her; there weren't many entries in the book and most of them were local.

'I'm going to phone round these numbers,' she thought. She sat up on the edge of her bed. But how was she going to do the telephoning. The only telephone was in the hall and Mum would hear her.

Sarah looked out of her window. Mum and James were at the end of the garden. Mum was struggling to clip the hedge and James was busy playing in his sandpit. Sarah decided to grab the chance; she ran downstairs, clutching the book tightly in her hand. She crouched at the bottom of the stairs. No one could see her there.

Nervously, Sarah dialled the first number in the book. Brr brr, brr brr . . . the ringing tone went on for ages.

At last someone answered. Sarah cleared her throat:

'Please may I speak to Stephen Jones?'

'Who?'

'Stephen Jones.'

'Sorry love, wrong number. No Stephen Jones here.'

Sarah put the phone down. She tried the next number.

'Eh? Never heard of him!' The phone was slammed down.

Sarah frowned. Surely, if Dad knew these people, they must know him – or at least know his name?

She tried two more numbers, but she got just the same replies. Sarah went into the living-room and peeped out of the window. Mum and James were still at the far end of the garden. Then, as she turned to go back to the phone, she suddenly remembered something. Something that had happened a few days before Dad disappeared.

Sarah sat down and put her hands

to the side of her head. It had seemed nothing at the time. She only remembered now because it had all happened here, just by the telephone.

It was just before Dad disappeared. She and James had been watching television. The phone rang and Sarah had answered it. But before she'd had time to speak, a harsh voice had barked, 'Mick?' at the other end of the line. Sarah told the caller he'd got the wrong number, put down the phone and went back to the television.

Just then, Dad had come in.

'Who was that on the phone?' he asked.

Sarah was watching one of her favourite programmes and she answered without looking up.

'Oh, just a wrong number. They wanted someone called Mick.' Dad said nothing, but Sarah heard a sharp intake of breath. She looked up. Dad was standing absolutely still, just by the door. His face was very pale. He hesitated, as if he wanted to say something, then he turned and went out.

Sarah went over and over this tiny incident. Perhaps it was nothing? Perhaps she had imagined that Dad had looked shocked when he heard the name Mick. But she had nothing else to go on. There was no other clue to Dad's disappearance. All she had was this address book and an idea that out there somewhere was someone whom Dad was afraid of. Someone who called him 'Mick'.

She looked out of the window again and saw her mother wipe her hand across her brow. James was tugging at her leg, wanting her attention. It wouldn't be long before they came into the house again. She wanted to tell Mum what she was doing, but she knew Mum would forbid it. She remembered Dad's note: '. . . don't try and find me or go to the police. If you do, you will never see me again.'

Sarah shivered. Then she took a deep breath and dialled the next number: 'Hello. Please can I speak to Mick?'

'No Mick here, dear. You've got the wrong number.'

The next two numbers were the same – no one called Mick. Sarah could hear James clamouring for a drink, and her mother's reply: 'Just one more minute, then we'll go in.'

Just one more phone call, thought Sarah. She dialled the next number in the book. This time the phone was answered almost immediately. 'Yes?' The voice was quiet but harsh. Sarah's voice was trembling, but she managed to get the words out:

'I want to speak to Mick. It's very important.'

There was silence at the other end. Silence that seemed to go on and on. Then at last, a reply:

'Who is this?'

Sarah suddenly felt very frightened. She put the receiver quietly back and wiped her hands down the sides of her jeans, as if, by speaking to

the person with that harsh but deadly, quiet voice, she had been somehow made dirty. She suddenly wanted to cry. She turned and stumbled out of the hall, knocking the telephone to the floor. When she knelt down to pick it up, she realized she was shaking all over.

She went to the back door, needing some fresh air. Everything looked so ordinary. The garden, the hole in the fence, the slide, her mum and James coming in, hand in hand.

But Sarah knew she had stumbled on to something far from ordinary. That voice on the phone was evil. It was a voice that came from a world that cared nothing for Mum and Dad or her and James or jam for tea or treats on Sundays. That voice had frightened her; it had frightened Dad, even. She wanted to run to Mum and tell her everything. But she couldn't; Mum was the last person who must know.

'. . . don't try and find me or go to

the police. If you do, you will never see me again.'

Mum smiled as she came towards her, pulling off her gardening gloves. 'Phew, it's hot work,' she said. 'Let's all have something to drink.'

Chapter Three

Sarah couldn't stop thinking about that harsh voice on the end of the telephone. She was sure it was the voice of the person who had phoned Dad and asked for Mick. Written in Dad's address book, against the number she had just phoned, was a name – Kevin Bradshaw – but it meant nothing to her. She'd never heard Dad talk about anyone of that name. There was an address, too, twenty-three Lindsey Street. Sarah knew that Lindsey Street was not far away – it was somewhere just the other side of the park.

Once or twice during the afternoon, the phone rang. Sarah jumped. But it was Mum's friends. Sarah listened to her mother: 'Yes. Stephen's away just now. No . . . no, I'm not sure. He's gone after a job. Yes, he'll be back in a day or two.'

Sarah could see her mother's hands while she talked on the phone. She twisted her wedding ring round and round her finger as she spoke.

How long can she keep this up, thought Sarah. How long can *I* keep it up, come to that, she added, to herself. She hadn't told anyone that Dad had gone away. Her best friend, Jenny, knew that Dad had lost his job – so did her teacher, Miss Appleby. But neither of them knew he'd left home.

Sarah's thoughts were interrupted by Aggie, jumping up, demanding attention. Aggie missed Dad as much as anyone. Dad used to take her for walks in the evenings, across the park, then over to the pub and back home.

The park! Lindsey Street was just the other side of the park.

'Mum,' said Sarah.

'Yes?'

'I'm going to take Aggie out to the park.'

'That's a good idea. Can you take James, too?'

'Oh Mum! I want to have a good long walk. He'll hold me up. I'll take him another time.'

But James had heard. 'I want to go *now*!' he whined.

'Look,' said Sarah, 'I'm just going to walk. I'm not going to the swings or the slides.'

Then she saw his face: 'I'll take you tomorrow – promise.' James bellowed, so Sarah got Aggie's lead and fled out of the front door.

Aggie knew exactly where they were going. The moment they turned out of the gate, she tugged at her lead, giving little yelps of pleasure. Sarah was towed along behind, deep in thought.

For the hundredth time, she asked herself the same questions: How could her dad leave them? How could he make Mum so unhappy and force her to tell lies? It must have something to do with that voice . . . that voice would scare anyone. Perhaps Dad was being kept somewhere against his will. Perhaps, perhaps, perhaps . . . It was not knowing that made it so awful. If only they knew where he was . . .

Aggie was pulling even harder now. Sarah had been so lost in thought that she hadn't realized they'd reached the park. She took off Aggie's lead and watched the little dog tear away across the grass, chasing imaginary rabbits and bouncing at birds. Sarah smiled. When Aggie had sniffed all the interesting smells in the park, she came back to Sarah and demanded more attention. Sarah threw sticks and watched as Aggie flung herself after them, so fast that she overshot where they landed, skidded to a halt and had to turn round to retrieve them.

At last, when they were both exhausted, Sarah put the lead on and Aggie turned immediately towards the pub.

'Not that way, Aggie,' said Sarah, pulling her firmly back. 'We're going somewhere different today.'

Puzzled by the change of routine, Aggie trotted after Sarah as they left the park by the far gate and walked down unfamiliar streets. I'm sure I've seen Lindsey Street somewhere near here, thought Sarah. She wandered up and down but all the streets looked the same and it wasn't long before she forgot the way she came. She was completely lost. Trying not to panic, she looked round for someone to ask. There weren't many people about, but at last she saw a lady with some shopping. 'Oh yes, dear,' she said. 'Lindsey Street. It's ever so hard to find.' And she gave her directions.

It was about half an hour since they'd left the park and at least an hour since they'd left home; Sarah knew that Mum would start worrying if they didn't get home soon. But she was determined to find the house in Lindsey Street, now that she had come so far. At last she found it. Number twenty-three Lindsey Street was exactly the same as the terraced houses on either side of it. Sarah was disappointed – she had expected it to be different somehow.

On the other side of the street, opposite the house, there was a low garden wall. Sarah sat down on it and Aggie flopped at her feet. Sarah felt rather stupid. Now that she'd found the house where this Kevin Bradshaw man lived, she didn't know what to do. Aggie knew what *she* wanted to do. She wanted to go home and have her supper. After a while she started to whine.

'Shh, Aggie, shut-up. I'll take you home soon.'

But that wasn't so easy. Now that she'd got here, Sarah wasn't sure how to get back to the park from Lindsey

Street. She had just decided to get up and go and find someone to ask, when there was a movement from across the street. A man was coming out of number twenty-three. Sarah froze; she tried to be as still and quiet as possible so he wouldn't notice her.

But Aggie had seen something else. Behind the man were two large Alsatian dogs. Aggie hated Alsatians. She growled.

'Be *quiet*!' whispered Sarah. Aggie growled louder.

The man didn't seem to notice them. But the Alsatians did. They strained at the leash, trying to come over the other side of the road and deal with Aggie. The man swore at them. Even from across the road, that harsh, deadly voice could only belong to one person. He glanced briefly across at Sarah and Aggie, then he hauled the Alsatians to heel and they all walked away.

Sarah shivered. She had never seen the man before, but she would certainly recognize him again. He was powerfully built, with dark, thinning hair, a big beaky nose and eyes that were too close together. He wore a dark blue anorak and carried a heavy stick.

She watched the man and his dogs until they turned the corner, then she and Aggie followed them. They must be going to the park. She kept them in sight and, sure enough, after only a few minutes, she saw the park gates. She looked at her watch: half-past five.

'I wonder if he goes to the park every day?' she asked Aggie.

For an answer Aggie, knowing she was going towards home and food, pulled hard on the lead. Sarah leant down and patted her. Then, taking the road round the edge of the park, they ran all the way home.

That night Sarah dreamt about her father again. It was almost the same dream as before. Again they were in the country, kept apart by a crowd of people. Sarah kept calling out, 'Dad, Dad, wait for me. I'm coming.' But her dad got further and further away from her. And this time, before he disappeared, he turned round to look at her. But when she saw his face, it wasn't her father after all. The beaky nose, dark hair and close set eyes were unmistakeable. The face belonged to Kevin Bradshaw – the man with the dogs.

Chapter Four

'You're very quiet this morning,' said Jenny. It was Monday morning and she and Sarah were sitting on the school bus.

'What?'

'What's the matter with you? You've hardly said a word – and you haven't been listening to me, either.'

'Sorry Jen. Look – I've got something important to tell you.'

Jenny moved nearer, 'Yeah – what?'

'I can't tell you here. It's really secret. I'll tell you at breaktime.'

Sarah had been thinking so much about her dad that she'd forgotten all about the school play. But Miss Appleby certainly hadn't. Over the weekend, she had worked out a list of costumes and a schedule of rehearsals. She handed a copy of the play to Sarah, with her part marked in:

'Now Sarah. There's a lot to learn. Do you think you can manage?'

Sarah nodded. During the morning they read through the play and started working out where people stood and where they came off and went on. Sarah became completely absorbed in it. She almost forgot about Dad for a while.

At breaktime, she and Jenny walked over to the far side of the playground, where no one could overhear them.

'Now,' said Jenny. 'What's this great secret, then?' So, sitting on a wall, in the corner of the playground, Sarah told Jenny everything. About Dad's address book, about Kevin

Bradshaw, about the telephoning and the house in Lindsey Street. When she had finished, she found she was crying.

Jenny put an arm round her shoulders. Sarah sniffed, 'I don't know what to do, Jen.'

'Shouldn't you tell your mum?'

'I can't, Jen. If she knew I'd found out about Kevin Bradshaw, she'd be worried sick.'

'You see,' she went on, 'Mum trusts Dad. He left that note saying she mustn't tell anyone or go to the police. If Mum thinks I'm trying to find Dad, she'll stop me. I know she will.'

'What are you going to do next?'

'I don't know.'

'Do you want me to help you?' asked Jenny.

Sarah smiled through her tears. 'If there were two of us, I wouldn't feel so frightened.'

The bell went for the end of break. Jenny got up and straightened her skirt. 'I'll come round to your house after school,' she said, 'and we'll make a plan.'

Jenny only lived a few streets away, so she was at Sarah's house just as soon as she had had something to eat. Sarah had invited her to tea – but she was quite glad when Jenny refused; Mum was finding it hard enough to feed her and James.

She and Jenny tried to make some plans, but James kept interrupting. He said he was an aeroplane and that he needed to take off and land in different rooms.

'Look,' said Jenny, when James had burst in on them again, 'let's take James and Aggie to the park. We can talk on the way there.'

Sarah looked nervous: 'We might see the man with the dogs.'

'Well, if we do, we might find out more about him,' said Jenny.

'I don't think I want to.'

'Oh, come on,' said Jenny.

Sarah went into the kitchen: 'Can we take James and Aggie to the park, Mum?'

Mum looked up from the sink and smiled. The sadness behind her eyes made Sarah want to cry.

'Yes, love, of course you can. But don't be late. And don't lose either of them!'

Sarah grinned: 'I might try and lose James!'

There had been such a row in the house, with Aggie yapping and James roaring in and out of rooms, slamming doors and making take-off and landing noises, that it was a relief to be out of doors. They set off down the street, Aggie straining at her lead and James well ahead of them, swerving from side to side, arms out, still a noisy jet aeroplane.

As they got to the park, Sarah looked at her watch. Half-past five. She looked nervously round, but there was no sign of Kevin Bradshaw or his dogs. Sarah relaxed and they all walked over to the swings and slide. James stopped being an aeroplane and turned into a racing driver; he ran to the top of the slide, sat there with his legs straight out in front of him, put his hands round a make-believe steering wheel and shot down making loud exhaust sounds.

Sarah and Jenny laughed at him and Aggie barked at the bottom of the steps, not quite daring to climb up and join him. James enjoyed having an audience, and he showed off more and more. Then, rushing to get up the steps, he tripped and tumbled to the bottom. He wasn't badly hurt, but he suddenly wanted his mum. Sarah picked him up and cuddled him and inspected the grazed knee. James stopped yelling and sucked his thumb. He was, after all, only four.

'I want to go home,' he said. Sarah put him down and took his hand. 'We'll go home in a minute,' she promised. 'Where's the ball?' she went on. 'Let's see if Aggie can fetch it.'

After a few minutes, James had forgotten his sore knee and was laughing at Aggie, who streaked after the ball, even if he only threw it a few metres. Sarah and Jenny sat on the swings and watched them.

'What are we going to do about your dad?' said Jenny as she pushed herself gently to and fro.

'I suppose . . .' began Sarah. But she got no further. In the distance, two large Alsatians were bounding into the park from the opposite gate. She grabbed Jenny's arm: 'Jen, I think those are his dogs!' The girls stared at the dogs. It seemed, at first, as if they were on their own. Then, round the corner came two men. One was very fat, with an untidy shock of sandy hair, and the other was Kevin Bradshaw.

'That's him!' whispered Sarah. 'The one in the dark blue anorak with the stick.'

The two men were deep in conversation. They walked slowly. Kevin seemed to be doing most of the talking. They took no notice of the dogs and they went towards a park bench and sat down.

Sarah shivered: 'Let's go, Jen. I'm frightened.'

'No,' said Jenny, 'Now you've got a chance to find out more about this Kevin man. Let's go closer and see if we can hear what they're saying.'

Sarah looked horrified: 'Jen, I couldn't! Anyway, he'd recognize me. He saw me watching the house yesterday. He'd be sure to suspect something if he saw me here today.'

'Of course he wouldn't. What's there to suspect, anyway?'

Sarah fiddled with the seat of the swing: 'Well – there's the phone call. He must be wondering who made the call and asked for Mick. I'm sure it won't be long before he realizes it's me and that I'm Dad's daughter. Especially if he keeps seeing me.'

Jenny jumped off the swing. 'We may never get another chance like this,' she said. 'If you won't go, then I will. There are some trees behind that bench. I could creep up behind them and listen.'

'Jenny – you *can't*.'

'Just watch me!'

Sarah felt sick. Everything seemed to be happening in slow motion. James throwing the ball for Aggie; Aggie running to fetch it; and Jenny walking, slowly but surely, to the other side of the park, towards the bench where the two men sat. Sarah tried not to watch her friend, but she couldn't help herself. Her heart thumped and her hands were clammy as she held tightly onto the sides of the swing, still moving to and fro, to and fro.

There were other people in the park. Other children playing, other people out walking their dogs. But Sarah was only aware of Jenny and of the two men on the bench. As she watched, Jenny melted into the trees which ran behind the bench.

Nothing happened.

There were shouts from other children, barks from other dogs, but the men never looked up – and they were still talking.

Sarah had been staring so hard towards the bench, that she didn't hear James at first:

'Sarah. SARAH!'

She looked up then. James was standing just beside her, one small fist rubbing his eye.

'What's the matter?'

James sniffed: 'Aggie's gone.'

'What!' Sarah got off the swing and started looking all round the park for Aggie.

But it was James who spotted her first. He pointed. 'Look – there she is!' Aggie had seen the two Alsatians. She was racing towards them, looking for a fight.

'Oh no,' gasped Sarah. 'Stay here, James,' she shouted. 'I'm going to get her.' She raced across the grass, but she was never going to catch Aggie.

The Alsatians had stopped sniffing about near the two men. They had seen Aggie and now they were heading towards her. There were two of them – and they meant business. 'AGGIE!' yelled Sarah as she ran, stumbling, towards the three dogs. But Aggie ignored her.

Suddenly, the Alsatians speeded up. The three dogs met. There was a furious growling and yelping and a blur of fur, legs and teeth.

Sarah had just got to the dogs when there was a shout. Kevin Bradshaw was standing up and screaming at his dogs. Even in the middle of the fight, his dogs knew that voice. He strode towards them, his stick raised. They left Aggie alone and slunk back to him.

Sarah knelt down beside Aggie. The little dog wasn't badly hurt, but if the Alsatians had had a moment more, they would have killed her. Sarah picked her up. As she stood up with the dog in her arms, she knew

that Kevin Bradshaw was nearby. She could feel his presence. Every nerve in her body was aware of him. She turned round slowly. He was bending down, putting his dogs on the leash. As he straightened up, he looked at Sarah with cold, expressionless eyes. Then he jerked his dogs to heel and walked away. He had looked long and hard. He would certainly know Sarah again.

Sarah ran back to the swings, still holding Aggie. To her great relief, both James and Jenny were there waiting for her and they left the park as quickly as they could.

'How did you get back to the swings?' asked Sarah, once they were clear of the park and she had got her breath back. Aggie had recovered and was trotting, rather soberly, beside them. Even James was quiet.

'When I saw the Kevin man get up to go to the dogs, I ran for it. I don't think they heard me. They were both too busy looking at the dogs.'

'Did you find out anything?'

Jenny nodded. She looked over her shoulder, but they hadn't been followed. 'They *did* talk about Mick,' she said. 'The Kevin man said that Mick was safe. They'd got him at the cottage at Avonlea.'

'Avonlea? Where's that?'

'Search me,' said Jenny, 'I haven't a clue. But wherever it is, they're going there this weekend.'

Chapter Five

They walked home quite slowly; even
James had stopped being noisy. He
held Sarah's hand and scuffed his
shoes along the pavement. He kept
looking at Aggie.

'Is Aggie all right?' he asked.

'Yes, she's fine, she just wants her
supper,' said Sarah.

'Was she frightened of those big
dogs?'

'Yes,' said Sarah patiently, 'I expect
so.'

'Why did they bite her?'

'Because she ran over to them

and growled.'

'Why did she growl at them?'

'Oh *I* don't know, James,' said Sarah crossly. Jenny came to the rescue. 'Look, James, there's a big yellow digger over there. Let's go and have a look at it.'

They spent a long time looking at the digger, but at least it made James forget the dogs. Sarah looked at her watch:

'Come on, we must get home. Mum will start to worry.'

They ran the rest of the way and arrived, out of breath, at Sarah's house. There was a familiar car parked outside.

'That's Miss Appleby's car,' said Jenny.

Sarah slowed up. She felt uneasy. She liked her teacher and she knew that Miss Appleby realized something was wrong; Sarah had been forgetting things recently. Because she'd been worrying about Dad all the time, she'd not been concentrating on her school work. She knew she wasn't doing very well – and yesterday, Miss Appleby had asked her if everything was all right at home.

'Yes, fine,' Sarah had said. But she had blushed, too.

Miss Appleby had never been to her house before. What was she doing here now?

Sarah, Jenny and James walked in the gate and down the path towards the back door. Just then, the door opened and Miss Appleby came out. Mum was saying goodbye to her.

'Hello!' said Miss Appleby to the children, then, to Sarah, 'Your mum has said she'll help make some of the costumes for the school play, Sarah. It's very kind of her.' Then she went on, 'And we've another idea, too.'

'What's that?' asked Sarah.

'Your mum will tell you,' she said, smiling. Then she walked down the path and got into her car.

'Bye Sarah, Bye Jenny. See you both in the morning!' James was standing at the gate, peering at the car. He waved his hand. Miss Appleby started the engine and waved back at him, 'Goodbye, James. You'll be starting school next term, won't you?'

James nodded. He felt very important.

Later that evening, Sarah was feeding Aggie. James was in bed and Jenny had gone home. Ever since Miss Appleby had left, Mum had been really cheerful. She was humming as she cleared up in the kitchen.

'What did Miss Appleby want?' asked Sarah.

'She's really nice, that teacher of yours,' said Mum. 'I'm glad she called round.'

'Yes. But why did she come? She could have sent a message about the costumes.'

Mum took off her rubber gloves and put them carefully on the edge of the sink. She pulled out a chair and sat down at the kitchen table.

'Well,' she began. Then she started fiddling with her wedding ring. Sarah waited.

Mum went on. 'She knows about Dad being out of work and things not being very easy.' She looked up. 'You told her, didn't you?'

Sarah nodded.

'Well,' said Mum. 'We got chatting and I told her that I used to be a secretary before I had children, and it appears the school needs a secretary next term. She wondered if I'd be interested in the job!'

She looked anxiously at Sarah. 'Would you mind if I worked at school?'

Sarah smiled. 'No . . . No, of course not. Anyway, we don't often see the school secretary.' She laughed. 'You and James and me could all go to school together.'

Mum looked serious. 'The money would be a real help, love.' Sarah nodded. She didn't need telling.

'But it wasn't just about the job,'

said Mum. 'She said you'd told her about selling the car and she wondered if we'd like to go out into the country one weekend for a picnic or something. She said one good turn deserved another and as I'd offered to help with the costumes, she'd like to take us all out for the day. Would you like that?'

Sarah smiled. 'Yes. It'd be good to have a day out.'

Mum sighed. 'It would be a real break.'

Sarah told Jenny at school next day. 'Miss Appleby's said she'll take Mum and me and James out for a day in the country one weekend.'

It was breaktime again and they were sitting in the corner of the playground. Jennie was busy examining her foot. 'That's nice,' she said. Then she held up her bare toe. 'Look, do you think that's a verruca?'

'Yuk!' said Sarah. 'Put it away!'

Jenny started putting on her sock.

It was half on when she let out a yell. 'Sarah! Don't you see what this means?'

'What? A verruca?'

'No, you idiot, Miss Appleby! A day out in the country!'

Sarah frowned: 'What are you talking about?'

But Jenny went on, stumbling over her words with excitement: 'Could you get your mum to ask her to take you this Saturday?'

'I don't know. Perhaps. Why?'

Jenny pulled on her sock and crammed on her shoe. She dragged Sarah up on to her feet.

'Where are we going?'

'We're going to find out where Avonlea is!' Jenny was already running back to the classroom.

Sarah began to understand. 'Jen,' she panted, as they went in through the school doors. 'Wait. It'll never work. Avonlea could be anywhere.'

'Well. It can't be that far away. It's worth a try.'

They found the big atlas in the classroom and Jenny thumbed through the index. 'Avon; Avondale; Avon Down. Avonlea!' Jenny jabbed her finger at the name. She turned the pages of the atlas. 'Here it is. It's not far away. And it's certainly in the country.'

Sarah peered over her shoulder. 'It's on the river too.'

Sarah and Jenny looked at each other.

'It would *have* to be this weekend wouldn't it,' said Jenny.

'But that's when Kevin Bradshaw said he was going there,' said Sarah.

'Yes, I *know*. But we'll have to risk it; we can't get there before the weekend. And afterwards, who knows? That Bradshaw man might move your dad or anything might happen. We want to get there as soon as possible.'

'But how could we persuade Miss Appleby and Mum to go to Avonlea. They may want to go somewhere else,' said Sarah.

'We'd better find out a bit about

Avonlea, then,' said Jenny.

'And we'd better find out if Miss Appleby is free this weekend.'

Sarah and Jenny asked everyone they knew about Avonlea. A girl in their class knew it. She said it was nice but there wasn't much to do; there was the river and places to picnic and a few antique shops.

'Miss Appleby likes antiques,' said Jenny. 'Someone who went to her house told me that she collects all sorts of old bits and pieces.'

'Mum would, too,' said Sarah, 'if she could afford them.'

It took a lot of persuading and a lot of arranging, but at last, the trip to Avonlea was set up.

'Why Avonlea?' asked Sarah's mum.

'Well,' lied Sarah, crossing her fingers behind her back, 'Miss Appleby really wants to go there and look at the antique shops.'

'Oh well,' said Mum, 'if that's where she wants to go, that's fine.'

But she looked a bit puzzled.

'Why Avonlea?' asked Miss Appleby, frowning.

'Well,' lied Sarah again, crossing her fingers tight, 'you see, Mum loves looking at antique shops, even though she can't afford to buy anything. She said Avonlea is full of antique shops and she'd really love to go there.'

'Oh well,' said Miss Appleby, 'It's her treat. If that's where she'd like to go, then we'll go to Avonlea.'

'And please,' said Sarah to Miss Appleby, 'Can Jenny come too?'

Miss Appleby smiled. 'Yes, dear, of course she can come, as long as none of you mind the squash.'

Chapter Six

Saturday morning came at last and Miss Appleby arrived at Sarah's house bright and early. Her car wasn't very big and she was right – it certainly was a squash! By the time they had packed in some picnic things, a few toys for James, Aggie, Mum, Jenny and Miss Appleby, there was hardly any room for Sarah. It was a warm day and James soon got restless.

'When are we going to get there?' he asked, when they'd been going only a few minutes.

'Quite soon, love. Let's play a game,' said Mum.

'They played all the car games they could think of, but the journey seemed to go on for ever. Aggie panted and the inside of the little car got stuffier and stuffier as they crawled through the Saturday traffic. But at last they left the town behind them and were out into the green fields. James cheered up.

'Look, there's a cow! And there's some sheep. Can we stop, Mum?'

'Very soon,' promised Mum. But it wasn't very soon. They drove on for another twenty miles or so. In the back of the car, Jenny whispered to Sarah, 'I hope it's going to be worth it when we get there!'

They reached Avonlea at last. It was a pretty village, and the river wasn't far away, but there wasn't much to do. There were a couple of antique shops, a post office, a few houses, a pub and a place that served cream teas. There were lots of other places, much nearer to home, where they could have had more fun.

'Isn't this lovely,' said Mum, determined to make the best of her day out. And she did look happy to be away from the town. She breathed in the fresh country air and stretched her arms.

'We'll take Aggie for a walk by the river while you look in the antique shops,' said Jenny.

'I want to come,' said James.

Mum saw Sarah's face, so she said, 'You come with Miss Appleby and me, James. You never know, we might find something in the shops for you!'

James allowed himself to be dragged off, and Sarah and Jenny ran towards the river, Aggie bounding at their side.

'We haven't got much time,' said Sarah. 'I said we'd meet them at twelve-thirty.'

They sat down on the grassy river bank; Jenny found a stick and threw it in and they watched its slow progress downstream until it rounded the bend out of sight. Then she turned to Sarah:

'We'll have to ask someone, but we can't go knocking on every door in the village.'

Sarah got up and looked about her. 'It seems so peaceful. I can't believe anything bad can happen here.'

They made their way slowly back up to the main street. They could see Mum and Miss Appleby chatting and laughing to a man in one of the antique shops.

There was a young woman pushing a buggy who was coming towards them.

'Er . . . excuse me,' said Sarah, keeping half an eye on Mum and Miss Appleby, 'We're looking for someone called Kevin Bradshaw. Er . . . I think he's got a cottage here.' As she said Kevin Bradshaw's name out loud, to a stranger, she felt a chill down the back of her neck.

The young woman frowned. 'I've never heard of him dear,' she said,

'And I know most people in the village.' Sarah felt almost relieved; they weren't going to have to see Kevin Bradshaw. But then she realized they wouldn't find Dad, either. All this way for nothing.

Jenny broke in: 'He's got two big dogs – Alsatians. Perhaps you've seen them?'

'Oh yes!' said the young woman. 'I know who you mean. I've seen the dogs, but I've never met your friend. But I think he must rent the keeper's cottage up there.' She turned and pointed towards the far end of the village. 'If you walk up past all the houses, you'll reach a track on your left. At the end of the track there is a cottage. Mind you,' she added, 'it's a long walk. It's a good way from the rest of the village.'

That sounds right! thought Sarah to herself. But aloud she said, 'Thanks very much. We'll go and see if he's there.'

The young woman smiled and

walked away, humming and pushing the buggy in front of her.

'Jen,' said Sarah, 'I'm frightened. Let's not go up there.'

'Don't be silly, Sarah. We won't let anyone see us. We'll just go and take a look.' She took Sarah firmly by the arm and they set off to find the track.

The track was overgrown, and if it hadn't been for some tyre marks which flattened the grass and nettles, it would have been very difficult for the girls to make any progress. As it was, they kept getting scratched by brambles.

'I wish I'd brought my wellies,' said Jenny, rubbing her leg. Aggie was whining. She was finding it hard-going, too. Sarah picked her up and they walked on. The trees on either side of them met overhead, making the path dark and gloomy. Sarah's heart began beating faster. Her hands were clammy and she held Aggie tight.

They walked on in silence. The

young woman in the village had been right. It was a long track and the further they went, the more dark and gloomy it became. There was a sudden rustle just by Sarah's feet. She jumped, her heart racing, but it was only a rabbit. Aggie saw it, too, and struggled out of Sarah's arms, barking and yelping with excitement. She dived into some brambles after the rabbit.

'Come here, Aggie. Stop making such a noise.' Sarah looked fearfully up the track, but there was no sign of life. It took ages, but at last Sarah and Jenny managed to retrieve Aggie. They were both scratched and stung and Sarah was close to tears.

'We shouldn't have brought her with us,' she said. 'She's going to ruin everything.'

The track seemed to go on for ever. The girls edged cautiously round every bend, expecting to see the cottage, but there was nothing except more track.

'It *can't* be much further,' said Jenny. 'How long have we been going?'

Sarah stopped and wiped the back of her hand across her forehead, then she looked at her watch: 'It's twelve o'clock already! If we're not back at twelve-thirty, Mum's going to get worried. What shall we do?'

Jenny looked uncertain. She was about to speak when there was a slight noise, quite close by. They stopped at once, hardly daring to breathe. The noise came again; a quiet cough. Sarah and Jenny looked at each other, their eyes wide. They stood absolutely still. Then a car door slammed and someone coughed again. It was so clear that it could only be a few metres away, just round the next bend. An engine started up.

'Quick,' whispered Jenny. 'Hide in the hedge!'

Ignoring the brambles and nettles, the girls pushed themselves into the hedge and crouched behind a thick

bush. But it didn't give them much cover. Aggie struggled, but Sarah held her tight. They heard the car approaching, bumping slowly down the track towards them and they clung together as it went past. If the driver had looked at the hedge, he would have seen them, but his eyes were on the track ahead, as he inched his way over the bumps and ruts. Cold, expressionless eyes. The eyes of Kevin Bradshaw.

When the car was out of sight, they crept out of their hiding place. They were both stung and scratched. Although the day was warm and, a few moments ago, Sarah had been too hot, now she started to shiver. She looked at Jenny.

'We were right,' she whispered.

Jenny nodded. She took Sarah's hand and gave it a squeeze. 'We must go on, Sarah. I'm sure your dad's there.' Sarah swallowed. She couldn't stop shivering, but she knew Jenny was right. They had come this far.

They couldn't give up now.

Hardly making a sound, they walked on the tyre marks made by Kevin Bradshaw's car. Round the very next bend, the track widened out into a clearing and in the clearing was a tumbledown cottage, backing on to some woodland. A broken fence surrounded it and swinging from the gate, held on by a piece of wire, was a sign, 'Keeper's Cottage'. Another car was parked in front of the cottage.

'This is it,' whispered Jenny. Sarah nodded. She couldn't speak. 'We can get to the back if we're careful. The trees should hide us,' said Jenny. Very carefully, they crept round to the back, keeping to the trees. Aggie was wriggling in Sarah's arms.

They found a place where they could see the back of the cottage without being seen themselves, then they settled down to wait. For ages, nothing happened. There was no sign of life.

'Shall we go nearer?' said Jenny at last.

Sarah shook her head. 'No, I'm sure there's someone there. They'd see us.' A few moments later, she was proved right. The back door opened and three men came out. Sarah and Jenny kept absolutely still, praying that Aggie wouldn't give them away.

They recognized the first man – he was the fat man Kevin Bradshaw had spoken to in the park. The second was a stranger with a shock of red hair, and the third was carrying a sackful of rubbish which hid his face from view. The man with the rubbish tipped the contents of the sack in a corner, rearranged it, and then struck a match and set light to it. The other men stood a little way behind him, watching.

The man setting fire to the rubbish sat back on his heels, but he still had his back to them. Then suddenly, Sarah felt Aggie stiffen in her arms. She yelped and tried to jump down.

The two other men didn't seem to hear the yelp, but the man lighting the rubbish did. He looked round sharply and at last they could see his face.

It was Sarah's dad!

Chapter Seven

Sarah couldn't help herself. She lurched forward, not caring if she made a noise, only wanting to run to her father.

'Dad!' she said, her voice hardly more than a croak.

Jenny pulled her back. 'You idiot,' she said fiercely. 'Shut up and keep your head down.' But it was too late. All three men had heard the noise and were looking around them. Aggie barked again, her tail wagging. Even from a distance she could recognize her master. Her bark was answered by a sudden explosion of noise from inside the cottage. The two Alsatians leapt up at the window. Aggie saw them and at once started growling, the hackles rising all along her back. For a moment, no one moved. Then the fat man who had been in the park started to walk towards the children's hiding place. Jenny was still holding on to Sarah:

'Quick! We'll have to run for it.'

Sarah seemed rooted to the spot. She was staring at her father. 'But Dad . . .' she began.

Jenny shook her. 'For goodness sake – run! That man saw us before, in the park. He might recognize us. Hurry!' But still Sarah didn't move. 'Sarah – we're no use to your dad here. We've got to get help. Come on!'

The fat man from the park was only metres away now. At last Sarah stumbled forward. They ran back the way they came, as fast as they could, dodging through the trees, not caring now how much noise they made. But

they were slowed up by Aggie who struggled all the time. They heard the fat man shout to his companion, 'You stay with Mick. I'll sort this out.' Then he started running after the girls. They broke out of the trees and started off down the track, stumbling, slipping, running blindly – desperate to get away. But the fat man was gaining on them. They could hear his laboured breath very close behind. Sarah was crying with fright. She felt as though her whole chest would burst.

'I can't go on, Jen!' she gasped.

Jenny looked over her shoulder. 'Try, Sarah. Please try! He can't last much longer. He's too fat to run far.'

Sarah's legs felt like lead. She forced them forward. Just as she knew she couldn't go on any more, Aggie finally wriggled from her grasp and jumped to the ground.

'Oh, no!' said Sarah.

'Don't look back,' said Jenny.

'I must get her.'

Sarah stopped and turned. For a few seconds she was face to face with the fat man. He was red from the effort of running and he lumbered nearer and nearer. He lunged forward to grab Sarah, but at that moment, Aggie flew at him, snapping at his leg and throwing him off balance. He lost his footing and fell heavily among the brambles and nettles.

Sarah just had time to pick up Aggie and get clear again before he heaved himself to his feet, swearing and shouting at them. But Jenny was right. He was unfit and not used to running. After a few more metres, he gave up and shouted abuse after them instead. The girls rounded two more bends and then slowed up.

'Do you think he'll come after us in the car?' panted Jenny. Sarah stopped and bent double, trying to get her breath back.

'I don't know. He might.' They started off again, jogging down the track towards the village. They were too frightened to notice the under-growth that whipped their bare legs.

'We'll have to tell someone now,' said Jenny. Sarah nodded. She felt sick with fright when she thought of her dad with those men. What would they do to him? And did they know who *she* was?

They were nearly at the end of the track when they heard the sound of a car. The overhanging trees and the tangle of hedge and undergrowth muffled the sound and they couldn't be sure where it came from.

'It's that fat man. He's coming after us in the car!' said Sarah. They started running again, as fast as they could, down towards the village.

'We're nearly there,' shouted Jenny. 'Once we're in the village we can . . .' But she never finished the sentence.

Bumping towards them, coming *from* the village, was a car. This time, there was no time to hide. It was Kevin Bradshaw and he saw them all too clearly. Sarah caught a glimpse of his face before she sprinted past the car, Jenny just behind her. If she had run fast before, that look made her move at double the speed.

They flew down the remainder of the track. Nothing happened for a few seconds, then they heard the sound of a car reversing back towards them. It couldn't go very fast over the bumps and ruts, but once it reached the road, they would stand no chance. The girls ran as they'd never run before, never stopping, never looking back. Even Aggie seemed to sense the urgency. Sarah had dropped her as soon as they got to the road, and now she was racing beside them.

Just as Kevin Bradshaw's car emerged from the track, they reached the first house in the village and dodged behind it. They watched as he drove slowly up and down the village street. At the far end, he got out and started to look more carefully.

'Where's . . . your . . . mum?'

gasped Jenny, as they stood flattened against the wall of the house, Aggie beside them, panting. Sarah's ears were singing and her whole body seemed to be heaving.

'I . . . said . . . we'd . . . meet . . . them . . . for a picnic . . . by the river,' she got out at last.

'We must find her quickly,' said Jenny. 'We'll have to make a dash for it. The river's over there – where we went before – down that path. You can't see it from here.'

Sarah crept to the edge of the house and peered round. 'There's no sign of him now – just his car.'

'Let's go then, quick!' said Jenny.

'Come on Aggie,' said Sarah. Keeping their heads down the two girls ran across the road, over a stile and on to the river path. Aggie kept up with them. They didn't dare look behind them so they didn't know whether Kevin Bradshaw had seen them or not.

They ran down the path and only

slowed up when they reached the river. Jenny was right. You couldn't be seen here from the village.

For a few moments, Sarah thought that her mother and the others weren't there. She felt panic rising; what would they do if they couldn't find Mum? Then she saw them, a little way off, sitting on a rug, the picnic things spread out all round them. With a last burst of energy, she and Jenny rushed over to them. Stepping in sandwiches and kicking over drink, Sarah flung herself into Mum's arms.

'You've got to help us,' she sobbed. 'We've found Dad!'

Chapter Eight

James jumped up. 'Where's Daddy, where's Daddy?' But Mum didn't seem able to take it in. She held Sarah close and looked over her head at Jenny.

'What? What does she mean?'

'It's true,' gasped Jenny. 'We've found him. He's up there in an old cottage with these awful men.' She pointed in the direction of the track. Gradually, the truth dawned. Sarah's Mum went very pale. Miss Appleby got up and took Jenny by the shoulders.

'What is all this, Jenny? What are you talking about?' Jenny looked round.

'We must hide somewhere. This man Kevin Bradshaw – he knows who we are. He's looking for us now. Oh *please*, Miss Appleby, *hurry*! We must get away.'

Miss Appleby frowned. 'But I don't understand. What is Sarah's dad doing here? I thought he had gone after a job somewhere . . .' She was interrupted by an awful shuddering sob. Sarah's mum had let go of Sarah. Her shoulders were shaking and she had covered her face with her hands. Sarah tried to comfort her.

'Please don't cry, Mum. It's going to be all right. I know it is. But we've got to get away from here and go to the police.' She and Jenny started to bundle up the rug and the mugs and sandwiches, not caring what got squashed or spilt in the process.

James started to cry, too. He was frightened; he'd never seen his mum

so upset and he didn't understand why all the picnic was being messed up. Sarah's mum wiped her eyes and, trying to control her sobs, she picked him up. Then she faced Miss Appleby.

'I've been worried sick,' she whispered. 'Stephen disappeared a month ago. He left a note saying I wasn't to tell anyone or we'd never see him again. I didn't know what to do.'

Miss Appleby thought for a moment. 'If the girls are really in danger, we must find somewhere safe to talk this over. Do you think that man in the antique shop would help us?' Sarah's mum nodded. 'Come on, then,' said Miss Appleby firmly. 'We'll put all the picnic things in the car and then we'll go and visit the man in the antique shop.'

'But what about Kevin Bradshaw?' said Sarah. 'He's up in the village looking for us.'

'Don't be silly, Sarah,' said Miss Appleby. 'Your mum and I will be with you. Nothing bad can happen.'

The sun was shining, the air was full of birdsong and the river wound lazily by. As they all walked back towards the road, Sarah put up a silent prayer. 'Please don't let anything bad happen to my dad.'

Kevin Bradshaw had seen the girls as they raced across the road and down the path to the river. He didn't follow them, but walked back to his car. He got in and drove for a few hundred metres, to a high point where he had a clear view of the river down below. He stopped the car and picked up a pair of binoculars; for a few moments he stared at the picnic party by the river, memorizing each face, then, quite slowly, he set down the binoculars on the seat beside him and drove off in the direction of the farm track.

When he reached the cottage, he spoke to the fat man. 'I saw two kids coming down the track just now. Did they come to the cottage?'

The fat man nodded. 'Yeah. But

they meant no harm. They were just walking their dog. I chased them away.'

Kevin looked at him coldly: 'One of those kids is Mick's daughter.'

'*What*! Are you sure?'

'Of course I'm sure. She looks just like him; anyway, we've seen her before – in the park at home. She's followed us here and this time she's brought the whole family.'

'What shall we do, Kev?'

For a moment, Kevin didn't answer. His cold eyes stared towards the cottage.

'Everything's all set for tonight?'

'Yeah. Everything's all set.'

'What about Mick. Did he see the kids?'

'I don't know. He seems a bit jumpy.'

'We need Mick. We can't do the job without him. Don't let him out of your sight. And pack up everything *now*. We'll move off early; Mick's kid might go to the police. We don't want them sniffing around here.'

The fat man nodded. 'We'll be ready in half an hour,' he said. Then he went into the cottage.

Kevin Bradshaw saw a snail on the grass. It was moving very slowly in front of him. He lifted his foot, then stamped on the snail, grinding it down until it was a mess of shell and slime. He smiled to himself, then he went in search of the other man – the man with red hair. When he found him, he gave him some instructions. This third man was slim and athletic, with arms like steel. He nodded while Kevin spoke to him, then he set off for the village by car.

The man in the antique shop was very surprised when Miss Appleby, Sarah's mum and the children all tumbled in and asked for his help. It took a long time to get the story straight. Sarah and Jenny told the others all about the notebook and the phone call and how they'd overheard

Kevin Bradshaw talking to the fat man in the park.

All the time they were talking, Mum sat with her head bowed, twisting her wedding ring round her finger. James sat on her lap and sucked his thumb.

'We must tell the police,' said Miss Appleby.

Mum looked up. 'But Stephen's note . . . !'

Miss Appleby knelt down beside her. 'Look,' she said gently, 'whatever he's done – whoever he's with – it's better that the police know.'

At last, Mum nodded silent agreement and Miss Appleby asked the antique man if she could use his telephone. He showed her into another room and she went through and shut the door.

There was a big old grandfather clock in the room where the others were sitting. It ticked loudly and it seemed to Sarah that the minutes were going past much more slowly than usual. No one said anything, but they were all aware of Miss Appleby's muffled voice coming from the next room.

At last, she came back. She was looking very serious. 'I've got a policeman friend at home,' she said. 'I've been talking to him and he's going to get on to the local police here. But he's going to run a check on Kevin Bradshaw first.'

'What do you mean?' asked Sarah.

'Well, he said the name sounds familiar. He thinks it may be a false name used by a well-known criminal. He's going to ring back in a few minutes.'

They sat in silence, all lost in their own thoughts. The grandfather clock ticked relentlessly on. Then the telephone rang and they all jumped. Miss Appleby went into the other room to answer it.

'I want a wee,' said James suddenly.

'I'll take him,' said Sarah, glad to get out of the room.

'It's down the passage, last door on the right,' said the antique man. Sarah took James by the hand and they went out. She showed him where the lavatory was and waited outside. The back door of the house was open and the sun streamed in from the garden. Sarah stood and looked out.

In the passage behind Sarah, a man emerged silently from the shadows. Suddenly, she was grabbed by arms like steel and, before she had time to cry out, a hand was over her mouth and someone was whispering in her ear, 'Come quietly, girl, or we'll kill your dad.'

Sarah could still just hear the grandfather clock ticking in the room where the others sat. Then she heard the lavatory flush.

But she was pushed forward, out into the garden, and then down a path. At the end of the path she stumbled, and one of her canvas shoes came off. Her captor took no notice but propelled her forward on to some rough ground behind the house to where a car was parked.

Chapter Nine

In a matter of seconds, the man had stuck a plaster over Sarah's mouth, tied her hands and feet and bundled her on to the back seat of the car. As they roared off, over the rough ground, then back up the village street, Sarah tried to think. But she was so frightened that her mind wouldn't work. She had a tickle on her nose, and she couldn't scratch it. In the end she slid down so that she was kneeling on the floor and could rub her whole face on the back seat.

They stopped, and Sarah guessed

that they had reached the track that led up to the keeper's cottage. The man got out of the car and slammed the door. Nothing happened, so very cautiously Sarah shuffled on to her knees until she could see out.

Before long, the other car came bumping down the track towards them. There were three men squashed into the front – Kevin Bradshaw, the fat man and Sarah's dad – and in the back were the two Alsatian dogs and some luggage and equipment.

The fat man got out and started to transfer some of the stuff into the car where Sarah was huddled on the back seat. There were cases and bags, but also a lot of heavy tools. Kevin Bradshaw sat in his car, drumming his fingers on the dashboard. Sarah's dad sat beside him. Sarah's dad was looking down. He hadn't seen her. Then, she was picked up and carried, trussed like a chicken, over to Kevin Bradshaw. Kevin wound down the window and looked out.

'Hey, Mick,' he said, turning to Sarah's dad. 'Look what we've got here!'

Then, at last, Sarah's dad raised his eyes and saw her. He let out an agonized cry and flung himself towards the door, fumbling with the handle, trying to reach her. But they were ready for him. There was a sinister click, and Sarah saw that the fat man had a gun in his hand. Her whole stomach turned over; she thought she was going to be sick – but she couldn't be sick; her mouth was covered with plaster. Dad slumped back in his seat but his eyes never left her face. Sarah started to cry; it was dreadful. The tears ran down her face and she couldn't wipe them away. She wanted to say, 'I'm sorry, Dad,' but she couldn't speak. She could only see the pain in his face.

'A little precaution, Mick,' said Kevin Bradshaw, the smile on his face never reaching the cold, expressionless eyes.

'Just in case you have any second thoughts.'

Dad's voice was scarcely more than a whisper: 'Don't hurt her. Please don't hurt her.'

'Don't worry, Mick. No one's going to hurt her. As long as you do your part of the job, no one's going to hurt her.' Then he paused and looked out of the window. 'Of course, if you try anything silly, then we might *have* to hurt her – just a little.'

Dad looked down. 'I'll do it. I won't cause any trouble, Kevin. Just so long as you let her go.'

'Sure, we'll let her go. After tonight, you can both go.' Then he added, in a very different voice. 'You are in it Mick – up to your neck. If you back out now, it'll be much worse for you – and your kid. We're not playing games. You knew all along what was happening. It's no good going soft now. It's too late.'

'But I . . .' Dad started.

'Shut up, Mick. We're wasting

time. Thanks to your stupid kid, we've got to move out in a hurry.' He turned to the other men. 'Come on. Get that gear shifted and shove the kid back in the car.'

Sarah was tossed into the front of the car and left there on her own. She stared across at the other car, willing her father to look at her, but he was holding his head in his hands. She watched the men. Kevin never moved from her father's side, but the others were changing the numberplates; it was obvious they had done it before.

With a sinking heart, Sarah realized that Kevin and his gang were going to get away. And that her dad was a part of that gang. Whatever they were going to do tonight, Dad was in it with them and they'd got her just to make sure he didn't back out. Once he'd done the job – whatever that was – he would be a criminal. Her gentle dad, a criminal!

If only the police would come; but she knew they would arrive too late now. Both cars were ready to go. Sarah looked round the car. Was there anything she could do to stop them? She shuffled nearer to the driver's seat. The keys were in the ignition. Keeping low, she pushed her body until her mouth was up against them. The plaster was right across her mouth, but she could move her lips slightly. She put her plaster-covered lips to the keys and just managed to get a grip on them. She jerked back, and groaned with pain; the movement had torn the skin under the plaster, but she had the ignition keys between her lips!

'Come on – let's get out of here!' Kevin Bradshaw's voice was impatient now.

'OK,' said one of the others, 'we're ready.'

Sarah looked round desperately. Where could she hide the keys? If only her hands were free! Then she noticed that one of the rear doors was still open – it must have been left open when she was taken out. Trying not to attract attention, Sarah pushed herself up so that she was kneeling on the front seat, facing the back of the car. She jerked her head in the direction of the back door and released the keys from her lips. She watched as, for an agonizing second, they balanced on the base of the door, before sliding off and down into a patch of nettles outside. Sarah dropped back into the front seat just as the man with red hair got into the driving seat beside her. He looked at the ignition and cursed. Then he got out again and started going through his pockets.

'What's up now?' shouted Kevin.

'Can't find my keys!'

The moments ticked by as he looked – on the floor in the car, in his pockets again, down the side of the seat.

'It's no good – they're lost!'

'Haven't you got spares?'

'Not here. They're back at home?'

All hell was let loose then. With swearing and cursing, the cases and heavy gear were put back into Kevin Bradshaw's car.

'We can't all get in one car!' said the fat man.

'There's no choice, you fool,' Kevin spat at him. 'We'll pick up another when we get clear.'

Sarah was left alone – trembling. They hadn't even suspected her! She had delayed them for a few minutes – but was that enough . . . ?

James came out of the lavatory, into the passage. Sarah wasn't there, so he wandered back to the room where his mum was sitting. He went and sat on her lap and looked at the huge clock in the corner. Miss Appleby was talking:

'The police are on their way now. They'll go straight to the cottage. If Kevin Bradshaw is who they think he is, they say he's very dangerous. They don't want any of us nearby. All we can do is sit and wait, now.'

A fly buzzed on the window and the

clock ticked – tick, tick, tick. Outside, the village street was deserted except for a tabby cat, washing itself in the sunshine. Aggie saw it and barked.

'Where's Sarah?' said Mum suddenly, jerking herself away from the terrifying thoughts which were racing round in her mind.

'Dunno,' said James.

'I'll go and find her,' said Jenny. She got up and walked off down the passage, then, when she couldn't find her in the house, she went out into the garden. Jenny suddenly started to feel frightened. Where could she be? She wouldn't have gone off on her own, would she? Then she saw something that made her go cold all over. At the edge of the path that led to some rough ground, she saw a canvas shoe – Sarah's shoe!

She ran back inside and exploded into the room:

'They've got Sarah! Kevin Bradshaw's got Sarah!'

*

They had finished cramming everything into Kevin Bradshaw's car and
the man with red hair had picked up
Sarah and was about to put her in,
too, when they all heard the noise.
Faint, at first, but getting louder. The
sound of several cars coming from the
village – and coming very fast. For
the first time, Sarah started to hope.
Would they get here in time? Please
let them get here in time!

She was thrown in the back and,
almost at once, the car moved off.
Kevin Bradshaw swung the wheel
round to the left and they roared off,
down the road, away from the village.

Suddenly, sirens began to wail.
Kevin put his foot on the accelerator,
flat on the floor. The car surged forward; the police cars were still some
way behind.

'If we keep this up, we'll get away,'
said the fat man. No one else spoke. In
the back, Sarah was being bruised
and bumped, crashing into tools and
cases, while the two Alsatians panted

down her neck. She could just see her dad's head, as he sat, squashed up, in front. But he didn't turn round. Suddenly Kevin swore, and then he shouted at the others.

'There's a road block ahead. Hang on. I'm going to try and go round it.' The car was wrenched round to the right. Up on to a bank and then down the other side. But Kevin hadn't seen the ditch. With a sickening lurch, the front wheels ploughed straight in. There was nothing they could do. They were stuck. The police at the road-block started to run towards the car, but the men were out in a flash. Kevin yelled, 'Bring the kid – and untie her so she can run. She could be useful.'

Bewildered, Sarah let someone slash the cords round her hands and feet and propel her in front. She started to run – blindly following the others. She felt something hard at her back and realized it was a gun.

'What about the dogs?' someone said.

'Leave them,' shouted Kevin. 'They're no use now.'

Sarah's stiff legs wouldn't obey her. She stopped once, to try and catch her breath, but was immediately pushed forward. But it was long enough for her to look around and she realized with a shock that she had been here before. When had she been here? Why was it all so familiar?

It was impossible to run fast with her mouth shut. Bracing herself, she gave a sharp tug. The plaster came off, and she yelled out in pain. Skin had come away from her lips and she could feel the blood trickle down her chin.

On she ran, conscious now that they were being chased. She tried to turn, to get to the police and safety, but a steel arm grabbed hers and pulled her onwards. But then, quite suddenly, the arm had gone, and there was the sound of barking dogs. Sarah stopped. At first she thought that the Alsatians had come with them after all. Then she realized what had happened. These dogs were police dogs – and they had pinned the red-haired man to the ground.

Sarah didn't know what to do. She could see her father, running ahead with Kevin and the fat man. Behind were the police. Suddenly, she knew why the scenery was so familiar. She *had* seen it before. She had seen it in her dream. The dream she had had twice; the dream when she saw Dad and called out to him.

With all the breath she could muster she yelled out, 'DAD! DAD!'

He was quite far ahead, but she knew he had heard, though he didn't turn round. 'DAD! COME BACK, DAD!'

She watched. He slowed up and then turned round and looked back at her. The fat man shouted something at him. Sarah's dad took no notice. Slowly he started to walk back towards Sarah. Sarah stumbled on to meet him.

The fat man raised his gun and a shot rang out in the summer air.

Sarah screamed and covered her eyes so it was a few moments before she realized that the shot had missed its mark. When at last she looked, the fat man was on the ground, hitting out with his gun at the police dog which had him pinned by the other arm. He was yelling hysterically at Kevin Bradshaw.

'You should have brought the dogs! You should have brought the dogs!'

But Kevin Bradshaw wasn't listening. He was some way ahead of the fat man, but a police dog was gaining on him and before long he, too, was pinned to the ground, shouting obscenities at the dog, the police and anyone else within earshot.

Sarah's dad never looked back, but he started to run. Sarah was running, too.

'Dad! Dad!' Sarah was sobbing now.

At last, they met, and for a few

moments they clung together. Then, arms round each other, they walked back to the waiting police.

Chapter Ten

It turned out that both the cars were stolen – and so were most of the tools. Kevin Bradshaw and the two other men were arrested and charged with theft, but the police had been looking for them for a long time in connection with some much more serious crimes.

There was no escaping the fact that Sarah's dad had known what was going on – even if he hadn't realized at first. So he was arrested, too, though he was later released on bail.

But it was a very long time before

the rest of his family learnt the whole truth. Dad had gone into a pub one evening – a pub near Lindsey Street where no one knew him. He was at the bar, making his half pint last as long as possible, when a stranger started talking to him. Before long, Dad found he was telling this complete stranger all about himself – how he couldn't find work, how he was always short of money and how difficult it was to pay bills.

'What's your name?' asked the stranger.

'Mick,' said Dad, wanting to be anonymous.

'I tell you what, Mick,' said the stranger, 'I'll lend you some cash to keep you going. You can pay me back when you like.'

One thing led to another and it wasn't long before Dad found he owed a lot of money to the man, money he could never hope to repay. But the man never seemed to worry about it. Until, one night, when he said, 'I'd like you to do me a favour, Mick.'

'Sure,' said Dad. 'Anything you like.'

'There'll be some money in it for you,' said the man.

And that was how it all started. Before long, Dad was involved in planning what would have been a very clever bank robbery. At first, he didn't realize what was happening and, when he did, he tried to back out. But the man wouldn't let him. He forced him to write the note to Sarah's mum, then drove him up to Avonlea, where he was kept under guard.

The man's name was Kevin Bradshaw.

It was nearly the end of term and the night of the school play. Dad had said he couldn't come; he was ashamed because everyone knew what had happened and he didn't want to embarrass Sarah. Sarah pleaded – so did her mum – but they couldn't change his mind.

The curtain was about to go up. Sarah peered through a hole at the audience. The lights had been turned off and it was very dark, but she thought she could see her mum. Yes, there she was! And there was the empty chair beside her. Sarah bit her lip. I wish he'd come, she thought.

Her cue came and she made her first entrance. After a few seconds she forgot everything except the play. She acted her heart out.

At the interval, she peered through the curtain again. He was there! He'd come after all! She found Jenny:

'Dad's come!' she said. Jenny squeezed her hand.

'Give it all you've got,' she said.

Sarah acted as she'd never acted before. She did it all for Dad.

As the cast took their curtain call, the audience burst into applause.

And Dad clapped hardest of all.

THE END

TRICK OR TREAT

BY JON BLAKE

'He's going to kill me! Don't they realize?
He's going to kill me!'

Twins Jason and Annie are horrified to learn
that there is a plot to murder their sweet Aunt
May, with whom they are staying. Though they
have a pretty good idea who the villain is,
things really heat up when they find out the
actual time the murder is going to take place!
Have they taken on more than they bargained
for?

A witty and lively adventure that will keep
thriller fans glued to the edge of their seats!

SBN 0 440 862078

YEARLING BOOKS

SAM, THE GIRL DETECTIVE
THE CASH BOX CAPER

BY TONY BRADMAN

'You're the only one who can prove I didn't do it, Sam . . . *You've got to help me!'*

A missing cash box full of money. A classmate under suspicion of theft, and Sam the girl detective suddenly has her first proper client – Steven Greenstreet, her deadliest enemy!

It looks bad for Greenstreet. He had the opportunity *and* the motive. Can Sam solve the case and find the real criminal? And is there a connection with a series of local burglaries? Sam means to find out – and quickly!

SBN 0 440 862418

YEARLING BOOKS

JUMPING JACK

BY DAVID WISEMAN

'Jumping Jack' someone at the front of the class hissed and the rest of the class began to murmur, 'Jumping Jack, Jumping Jack...'

Jack doesn't like the look of his new school one bit. It's so old and spooky-looking that Jack is convinced it's haunted, and all the children in his class seem cold and unfriendly. Except one. A lively and mischievious girl in strange, old-fashioned clothes, who tells him her name is Jenny.

But there is a mystery surrounding Jenny. For one thing, nobody else seems able to see her! Could she possibly be a ghost? All Jack knows is that she is his friend and he is glad that she is there, helping him through the first awkward days. But it is only when one of his class mates is in desperate danger that Jack finally learns the real truth about Jenny...

SBN 0 440 862051

YEARLING BOOKS

THE CREATURE IN THE DARK

BY ROBERT WESTALL

'It stopped about ten yards away and looked at him steadily. Its eyes were a very pale green, as cold as ice.'

First Sammy and his father find a dead sheep. Then other animals die or go missing, and a great black creature is seen vanishing into the night. But what kind of monster could the killer be? Can anyone stop it?

Caught up in the middle of the dangerous excitement, Sammy is to need all his courage and determination when he comes face-to-face with the killer . . .

A tense, absorbing and action-packed adventure from an award-winning author.

SBN 0 440 862019

YEARLING BOOKS

DONNABELLA

BY MAGGIE PEARSON

Respectable Witch Seeks Familiar
No Experience Needed
As Training Given
Live In

When Donnabella the witch advertises for a familiar and gets Miss Plint instead, she little realizes the havoc that the well meaning lady will cause. There is the vanishing spell, for instance, and the shrunken spacemen, mistaken for garden gnomes . . .

SBN 0 440 862434

YEARLING BOOKS

If you would like to receive a Newsletter about our new Children's books, just fill in the coupon below with your name and address (or copy it onto a separate piece of paper if you don't want to spoil your book) and send it to:

The Children's Books Editor
Transworld Publishers Ltd.
61–63 Uxbridge Road,
Ealing
London W5 5SA

Please send me a Children's Newsletter:

Name . . . .

Address . . . .

. . . .

. . . .

All Children's Books are available at your bookshop or newsagent, or can be ordered from the following address:
Transworld Publishers Ltd.,
Cash Sales Department,
P.O. Box 11, Falmouth, Cornwall TR10 9EN

Please send a cheque or postal order (no currency) and allow 80p for postage and packing for the first book plus 20p for each additional book ordered up to a maximum charge of £2.00 in UK.

B.F.P.O. customers please allow 80p for the first book and 20p for each additional book.

Overseas customers, including Eire, please allow £1.50 for postage and packing for the first book, £1.00 for the second book, and 30p for each subsequent title ordered.